P9-DGQ-874

Walt Disney

DUMBO

Illustrated by the Disney Storybook Artists
Adapted by Kate Hannigan

Published by
Louis Weber, C.E.O.
Publications International, Ltd.
7373 North Cicero Avenue
Lincolnwood, Illinois 60712

Ground Floor, 59 Gloucester Place
London W1U 8JJ

Customer Service: 1-800-595-8484 or customer_service@pilbooks.com

www.pilbooks.com

p i kids is a registered trademark of Publications International, Ltd.

Manufactured in China.

ISBN-10: 0-7853-9543-1
ISBN-13: 978-0-7853-9543-0

On a dark night full of clouds, a flock of storks flew through the rain with special deliveries for the circus animals. The storks carried precious bundles in their long beaks: babies! There were twin bear cubs for Mrs. Bear, sweet tiger cubs for Mrs. Tiger, and a tall giraffe baby for Mrs. Giraffe.

Amid the excitement, a mother elephant anxiously watched the skies for her delivery. Mrs. Jumbo was hoping that she would get a baby, too. But the storks did not stop for her.

When the sun rose the next morning, Mrs. Jumbo and the other animals climbed aboard the circus train called Casey Jr. But one last stork still had a delivery to make. He was lost, so he sat on a cloud and looked at a map. Finally he spotted the circus train below and swooped out of the clouds with his heavy bundle in his beak. "Mrs. Jumbo!" he called. "I have a delivery for you!"

Mrs. Jumbo was delighted. She opened up the blanket, and there sat the most adorable baby elephant she had ever seen. He was just perfect.

The other elephants *oohhed* and *aahhed* over Mrs. Jumbo's baby. She smiled proudly and tickled him under his chin with her long trunk. *Ah-choo!* As the baby sneezed his ears flapped open. They were enormous!

The other elephants gasped. They pointed at the baby elephant's ears and whispered. Then they began to laugh. Mrs. Jumbo didn't think it was funny. She was angry at the other elephants. With her long trunk, she cradled her sweet Baby Jumbo.

"Jumbo?" said an elephant. "You mean Dumbo!"

The elephants laughed at the new name. Mrs. Jumbo shut her door and snuggled down in the hay with her baby. She loved Dumbo, ears and all. When Casey Jr. finally came to a noisy halt, Mrs. Jumbo and her baby went to work putting up the big top.

The next day was sunny and beautiful. The animals
marched through town on their way to the circus tent.
There were tigers and gorillas, camels and kangaroos. At
the end of the parade came the elephants.

Dumbo marched along excitedly behind his mother. He
felt like a star as everyone cheered and clapped. Suddenly
he stumbled on his ears and fell right into the mud.
Dumbo was a mess! The crowd laughed at him.

Mrs. Jumbo took her baby back to the circus tent and gave him a bath with her trunk. Dumbo was squeaky clean by the time the crowds arrived to watch the show. Some noisy boys stopped by the elephant stall and laughed at Dumbo. One boy even reached over and tugged on the baby elephant's big ears.

Mrs. Jumbo was very angry with the mean boy. She was so upset with the boy, the ringmaster had to take her away.

Dumbo was sad. He heard the other elephants talking. "Pretend you don't see him," they said, turning their backs on the baby elephant. Dumbo walked away all alone.

Timothy Mouse sat on a haystack nearby and watched. He felt bad for Dumbo and decided to do something about it. Timothy knew that elephants are afraid of mice, so he walked right over to the giant animals and waved his tiny paws. They were terrified!

Timothy laughed and told Dumbo he was his friend. He liked the baby elephant's big ears and thought he could be a star someday. Timothy thought Dumbo just needed the right act. Suddenly Timothy had a great idea.

Timothy scurried over to the ringmaster's bed and whispered Dumbo's name in his ear. When the ringmaster awoke in the morning, the first thing he thought about was Dumbo. That little elephant with the big ears would be perfect in the new circus act, the ringmaster said to himself.

That night as the circus began, the ringmaster proudly announced a new act called the Elephant Pyramid. In the center ring, one elephant climbed onto a big ball. Another elephant climbed on her back. Then another and another. Soon there was a wobbly tower of elephants teetering high above the crowd.

The audience cheered with excitement.

Dumbo was nervous. Every time he practiced his part of the new act, he tripped over his long ears. Timothy Mouse tried to help by tying Dumbo's ears in a knot. Suddenly the curtains opened, and the spotlight shone on Dumbo.

Timothy pushed his nervous friend forward, and Dumbo ran down the red carpet. Dumbo was supposed to spring into the air to the top of the elephant pyramid. But he tripped over his own ears again. Dumbo tumbled right into the ball that supported the tall tower of elephants. Down they crashed, bringing the whole circus tent down with them. It was a disaster!

Casey Jr. chugged home the next day, and the elephants complained the whole way. Their bodies were sore and their egos were bruised. They raised their trunks together and took a solemn vow. "From now on, Dumbo is no longer an elephant," they said.

The ringmaster felt the same way. Dumbo had made him look foolish, he thought to himself, so he would make Dumbo the fool. The ringmaster sent Dumbo to perform with the clowns.

Dumbo had to jump from a tower into a tiny bucket of water. The crowds laughed at the silly routine, but Dumbo felt embarrassed. He didn't want to be a clown—he wanted to be an elephant.

The clowns were glad to have Dumbo in their act, but they wanted to make him do more dangerous tricks. One clown warned that they should be careful not to hurt Dumbo. But the others just laughed. "Elephants don't have any feelings," they said.

That night, Dumbo and Timothy Mouse slept in a warm pile of hay. Dumbo dreamed he could fly. He flapped his ears and soared just like a bird. It was a wonderful dream, and it seemed so real.

When they awoke in the morning, Timothy Mouse looked all around. He shook Dumbo awake and asked him what had happened. They were high above the ground in the branches of a tree! Dumbo and Timothy were so surprised, they jumped. Down, down, down they fell into a pond of water. They could hear the laughter of some birds nearby.

Timothy thought they had flown up into the tree. But when Dumbo flapped his ears, he didn't leave the ground. The birds laughed even harder. Timothy Mouse looked at them and huffed. He was getting very impatient.

Finally the birds decided to help. They handed Timothy Mouse one of their black feathers. "Tell him it's a magic feather," they said to Timothy.

Timothy Mouse explained to Dumbo that the magic feather would help him fly. He led Dumbo to the edge of a tall rock, and then he climbed onto his friend's hat. Dumbo clutched the magic feather in his trunk and began to flap his ears. A big cloud of dust and dirt swirled in the air all around them.

Timothy was disappointed. He didn't think anything was happening. Once the dust settled, he looked down. Timothy couldn't believe his eyes. The ground was far below them. They were flying! They really had a great act for the circus now, Timothy thought.

Under the big top that night, the clowns performed their silly routine again. Only this time, they made Dumbo's tower even higher than before. It nearly touched the top of the circus tent.

Dumbo climbed the tall tower and looked down at the people below. They all seemed so far away. Timothy perched on Dumbo's trunk and tried not to get dizzy from the height.

When the trumpets blared, it was Dumbo's big moment.
He stood in the spotlight's glare and held the magic
feather in his trunk. Dumbo winked at Timothy on his
trunk and jumped from the tower. Suddenly the magic
feather slipped from his trunk.

Down, down, down they dropped. They were falling fast!

Timothy Mouse had to think quickly. He shouted in the
elephant's big ear, telling Dumbo the feather wasn't really
magic. "You don't need it," Timothy told Dumbo. "You
can fly all by yourself. Trust me!"

At the last moment, Dumbo flapped his ears. He really could do it—Dumbo could fly! He swooped over the heads of the people in the crowd and soared all around the big top.

The clowns were so surprised at the sight of him that they ran away. Dumbo laughed and scooped peanuts up in his trunk, spraying them down on the elephants who were so mean to him. The crowds cheered. They had never seen anything so amazing.

Dumbo was a sensation. People came from all around to see him and his magical, marvelous ears. Mrs. Jumbo returned and watched her baby fly around the circus tent. It was her proudest moment. From that day on, she and Dumbo were always together. The ringmaster even built a special rail car for them and hooked it onto Casey Jr.

Dumbo forgave the other elephants for being so cruel. His ears really did make him different. In fact, they made him a star.